Marigold's Bad Hair Day

by Margaret Nash

Illustrated by Martin Remphry

W

First published in 2010 by
Franklin Watts
338 Euston Road
London
NW1 3BH

Franklin Watts Australia
Level 17/207 Kent Street
Sydney
NSW 2000

A CIP catalogue record for this book is available
from the British Library.

ISBN 978 0 7496 9430 2 (hbk)
ISBN 978 0 7496 9435 7 (pbk)

Series Editor: Jackie Hamley
Series Advisor: Catherine Glavina
Series Designer: Peter Scoulding

Printed in China

Franklin Watts is a division of
Hachette Children's Books,
an Hachette UK company
www.hachette.co.uk

Marigold couldn't sleep. She tossed and turned all night long. She was too hot.

"It's my thick wool that's the problem," she told the others the next day. "I want it cut."

"You must wait for the
sheep shearer," they said.

"Not me," said Marigold.
"I'm not waiting!"
She flounced down to
the farm gate with her
head in the air.

She saw Taffy the sheepdog
lying on the grass, and told
him about her problem.

"I have a friend who cuts hair," he said. "She has a place in town. I'll take you there."

"TOWN!" cried Marigold.
"Fantastic!" Only posh animals
like the horse went to town.

"She does a very good job, they say," said Taffy as they walked down the street.

"WOW! Is this it?" said Marigold.

"Yes," said Taffy, "in you go!"

So Marigold walked in.

Madam Pomp stared at her.

"I don't do sheep," she said.

"I'm a friend of Taffy's," explained
Marigold. "He brought me."

"Oh, well! Any friend of Taffy's is a friend of mine," said Madam Pomp.

Madam Pomp pulled back the chair for Marigold. "Take a seat. Now what can I do for you?" Marigold looked round. "Well... er..." she said.

16

"I do short back and sides, long sides and back. I do fluffy tops, curly socks, pom-pom tails and polished nails," said Madam Pomp. Marigold blinked.

Madam Pomp looked at Marigold's hoofs. "Nails may be tricky," she said.

"I just want a good trim, please," said Marigold nervously.

"OK," said Madam Pomp. "Let's go!"

Madam Pomp got her scissors and snipped until there was a pile of wool on the floor.

Then she gave Marigold a mirror.

"That's not me!" gasped Marigold.

"It is," said Madam Pomp.

"Don't you look lovely?"

But Marigold had left the shop.
She was running home.

24

When she got back, there
was only Taffy in the field.
"Who are you?" he asked.
"It's me, Marigold!" she said.

Then Marigold ran to the barn to hide, but found all the other sheep there, being shorn.

They laughed loudly when they saw her. The farmer got his camera and took her picture.

"Your turn next, my girl," he said. Marigold sank gratefully against the sheep shearer's legs.

And she never visited Madam
Pomp again!

Puzzle 1

Put these pictures in the correct order.
Now try writing the story in your own words!

Puzzle 2

Choose the correct speech bubbles for each character. Can you think of any others? Turn over to find the answers.

Answers

Puzzle 1

The correct order is: 1d, 2e, 3a, 4f, 5c, 6b

Puzzle 2

Marigold: 3, 4

Madam Pomp: 2, 5

Farmer: 1, 6

Look out for more great Hopscotch stories:

My Dad's a Balloon
ISBN 978 0 7496 9428 9*
ISBN 978 0 7496 9433 3

Bless You!
ISBN 978 0 7496 9429 6*
ISBN 978 0 7496 9434 0

AbracaDebra
ISBN 978 0 7496 9427 2*
ISBN 978 0 7496 9432 6

Mrs Bootle's Boots
ISBN 978 0 7496 9431 9*
ISBN 978 0 7496 9436 4

How to Teach a Dragon Manners
ISBN 978 0 7496 5873 1

The Best Den Ever
ISBN 978 0 7496 5876 2

The Princess and the Frog
ISBN 978 0 7496 5129 9

I Can't Stand It!
ISBN 978 0 7496 5765 9

The Truth about those Billy Goats
ISBN 978 0 7496 5766 6

Izzie's Idea
ISBN 978 0 7496 5334 7

Clever Cat
ISBN 978 0 7496 5131 2

"Sausages!"
ISBN 978 0 7496 4707 0

The Truth about Hansel and Gretel
ISBN 978 0 7496 4708 7

The Queen's Dragon
ISBN 978 0 7496 4618 9

Plip and Plop
ISBN 978 0 7496 4620 2

Find out more about all the Hopscotch books at:
www.franklinwatts.co.uk

*hardback